Ladybird Readers

Little Red Riding Hood

Series Editor: Sorrel Pitts
Text adapted by Coleen Degnan-Veness
Illustrated by Diana Mayo

LADYBIRD BOOKS

UK | USA | Canada | Ireland | Australia
India | New Zealand | South Africa

Ladybird Books is part of the Penguin Random House group of companies
whose addresses can be found at global.penguinrandomhouse.com.
www.penguin.co.uk   www.puffin.co.uk   www.ladybird.com

Penguin
Random House
UK

First published 2016
003

Copyright © Ladybird Books Ltd, 2016

The moral rights of the author and illustrator have been asserted

Printed in China

A CIP catalogue record for this book is available from the British Library

ISBN: 978-0-241-25446-2

Little Red Riding Hood

Little Red Riding Hood

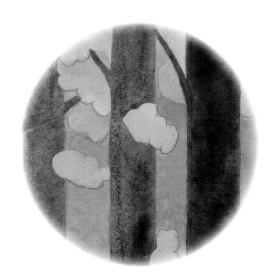

forest

wolf

knock

ax

Little Red Riding Hood
lived with her mother
and father in a
little house.

One day, Little Red Riding
Hood's mother said,
"Can you take these
cakes to Grandmother?"

"Yes," said Little Red
Riding Hood.

Grandmother's house was in the forest. And a wolf lived near it.

The wolf saw Little
Red Riding Hood.
"I want to eat her!"
he said. And he ran to
Grandmother's house.

Little Red Riding Hood knocked on her grandmother's door.

"Come in, Little Red Riding Hood!" said Grandmother.

Grandmother was in
the bed. But her face
was different.

"Come near to me, my
dear," said Grandmother.

"Oh, Grandmother," said Little Red Riding Hood. "You have got very big ears!"

"I can hear you very well with them, my dear," said Grandmother. "Please, come near to me."

19

"Oh, Grandmother," said
Little Red Riding Hood.
"You have got very big eyes!"

"I can see you very well
with these big eyes, my
dear," said Grandmother.
"Please, come near to me."

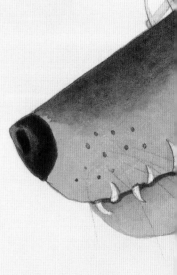

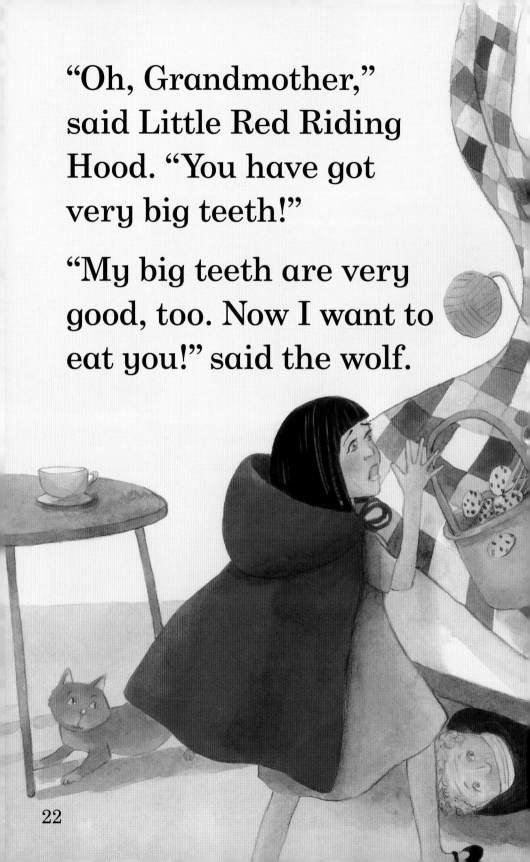

"Oh, Grandmother," said Little Red Riding Hood. "You have got very big teeth!"

"My big teeth are very good, too. Now I want to eat you!" said the wolf.

And the wolf jumped
from Grandmother's bed!

Little Red Riding Hood
ran from room to room.
"Help! Help!" she said.

Little Red Riding Hood's father was in the forest and he ran to Grandmother's door with his big ax.

The wolf saw the ax
and he jumped from
a window. He ran and
ran. Little Red Riding
Hood never saw him
in the forest again.

Activities

The key below describes the skills practiced in each activity.

Spelling and writing

Reading

Speaking

Critical thinking

Preparation for the Cambridge Young Learners Exams

1 Look and read.
Put a ✓ or a ✗ in the box.

1  This is Little Red Riding Hood. ✓

2  This is her mother. ☐

3  This is the wolf. ☐

4  This is her father. ☐

5  This is her grandmother. ☐

2 **Look and read.**
Write *yes* or *no*.

One day, Little Red Riding Hood's mother said, "Can you take these cakes to Grandmother?"

"Yes," said Little Red Riding Hood.

1 Little Red Riding Hood lived with her mother and father.

_____yes_____

2 Little Red Riding Hood's mother said, "Can you take these cakes to the wolf?"

_____

3 Grandmother's house was in a forest.

_____

3 **Work with a friend.**
Talk about the two pictures.
How are they different? 🗨

a   b

Example:

In picture a,
the wolf is not
wearing glasses.

In picture b,
the wolf is wearing
Grandmother's glasses.

4 Find the words.

e	a	t	g	h	f
n	x	u	r	o	o
k	f	o	a	r	r
n	z	n	n	s	e
o	w	i	d	e	s
c	v	e	m	h	t
k	z	q	o	m	b
s	o	u	t	w	m
a	a	t	h	h	e
c	n	c	e	o	a
b	a	i	r	w	l

eat

knock

forest

grandmother

ax

34

5 **Look at the pictures and read the questions. Write complete sentences.**

One day, Little Red Riding Hood's mother said, "Can you take these cakes to Grandmother?"

"Yes," said Little Red Riding Hood.

The wolf saw Little Red Riding Hood. "I want to eat her!" he said. And he ran to Grandmother's house.

1 Who made cakes for Grandmother?

Little Red Riding Hood's mother made cakes for Grandmother.

2 Who did the cakes to Grandmother?

....

3 Who did the wolf want to eat?

....

....

6 Look at the pictures. Talk to your teacher about Little Red Riding Hood's morning. 🗨

Example:

> *Little Red Riding Hood was in the garden . . .*

7 **Read the text. Choose the right words and write them on the lines.** 📖 ✏️ ✳️

1	has	had	have
2	must	can	had to
3	when	or	became

"Oh, Grandmother, you ¹ __have__

got very big ears!" said Little Red

Riding Hood. "I ² _____

hear you very well with them, my

dear," said Grandmother. Little Red

Riding Hood was very frightened

³ _____ she saw

Grandmother's big teeth.

8 **Look at the pictures. One picture is different. How is it different? Tell your teacher.** ●

1

a ![wolf picture a]

b ![wolf picture b]

c ![wolf picture c]

d ![wolf picture d]

> *Picture a is different because the wolf is not wearing Grandmother's clothes.*

2

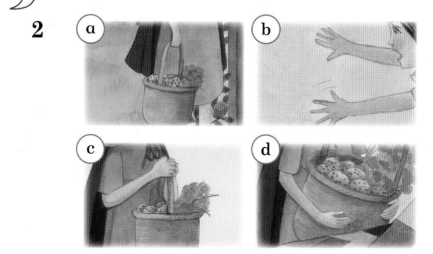

a

b

c

d

9 Look and read.
Write the answers. 📖 ✏️

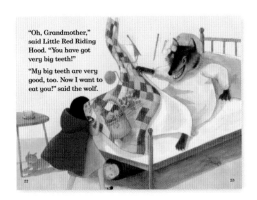

"Oh, Grandmother," said Little Red Riding Hood. "You have got very big teeth!"

"My big teeth are very good, too. Now I want to eat you!" said the wolf.

1 Why did the wolf wear Grandmother's clothes? **(eat / Little Red Riding Hood)**

Because he wanted to eat Little Red Riding Hood.

2 What did the wolf do to Grandmother? **(put / under the bed)**

3 Why did Little Red Riding Hood say, "Help! Help!"? **(be / frightened)**

10 **Write *always* or *never*.**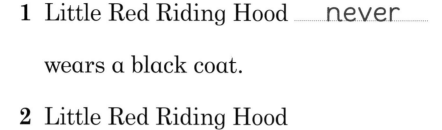

1 Little Red Riding Hood ___never___ wears a black coat.

2 Little Red Riding Hood _____ wears a red coat.

3 The wolf _____ talks to Little Red Riding Hood's father.

4 The wolf is _____ hungry.

5 Little Red Riding Hood _____ sees the wolf again.

11 **Ask and answer the questions with a friend.** 🗨

Little Red Riding Hood lived with her mother and father in a little house.

6

1 *What is Little Red Riding Hood's mother doing?*

She is cooking.

2 What is Little Red Riding Hood doing?

3 Is her father playing?

4 Is their house big or small?

12 **Read the text and choose the best answer.**

1 "Can you take these
cakes to Grandmother?"
a "Yes, of course."
b "No, thank you."

2 "Goodbye, Mother!"
a "Hello."
b "See you later."

3 "I have got some cakes
for you."
a "Don't worry."
b "Thank you, my dear."

4 "You have got very big ears."
a "I can hear you very well."
b "Now I want to eat you."

13 Write the missing letters.

ai   aw   ea   ee   oo

1 Little Red Riding Hood t o o k

the cakes to Grandmother's house.

2 The wolf s _____ Little Red Riding

Hood in the forest.

3 "Come in, Little Red Riding Hood!"

s _____ d Grandmother.

4 "Come n _____ r to me, my dear,"

said Grandmother.

5 "I can s _____ you very well with

these big eyes," said Grandmother.

14 **Circle the correct picture.**

1 Who enjoys making cakes?

2 Who does not have any friends in the story?

3 Who enjoys eating cakes?

4 Which person works with an ax?

15 Order the story. Write 1—5.

.... The wolf saw Little Red
Riding Hood. The wolf ran
to Grandmother's house.

.... The wolf saw Little Red Riding
Hood's father with his ax.
The wolf ran and ran.

___1___ Little Red Riding Hood's mother
made some cakes. Little Red
Riding Hood took them to
Grandmother's house.

.... Little Red Riding Hood knocked
on Grandmother's door.

.... The wolf jumped into
Grandmother's bed.

16 Ask and answer questions about the picture with a friend. 🗨

The wolf saw the ax and he jumped from a window. He ran and ran. Little Red Riding Hood never saw him in the forest again.

28

Example:

What is the wolf doing?

The wolf is running from Little Red Riding Hood's father.

17 Read the questions and answers.
Write *Where*, *Why*, or *Who*. 📖 ✏️

1 ___Where___ did the wolf see
Little Red Riding Hood?

He saw her in the forest.

2 _____ was in
Grandmother's bed?

The wolf was in her bed.

3 _____ didn't Little Red
Riding Hood go near the bed?

She was frightened.

4 _____ did Little
Red Riding Hood go to
Grandmother's house?

To give Grandmother some cakes.

Level 2

The Gingerbread
Man

978–0–241–25442–4 ☐

Sly Fox and
Red Hen

978–0–241–25443–1 ☐

The Monster
Next Door

978–0–241–25444–8 ☐

Wild Animals

978–0–241–25445–5 ☐

Little Red
Riding Hood

978–0–241–25446–2 ☐

Dinosaurs

978–0–241–25447–9 ☐

Topsy and Tim
The Big Race

978–0–241–25448–6 ☐

Peter Rabbit Goes
to the Treehouse

978–0–241–25449–3 ☐

Sports Day

978–0–241–26222–1 ☐

Going on a Picnic

978–0–241–26221–4 ☐

Now you're ready for Level 3!

Notes
CEFR levels are based on guidelines set out in the Council
of Europe's European Framework. Cambridge Young Learners
English (YLE) Exams give a reliable indication of a child's
progression in learning English.